Olof and Lena Landström

WILL GOES
TO THE BEACH

Translated by Carla Wiberg

R&S
BOOKS

Stockholm New York London Adelaide Toronto

Rabén & Sjögren Bokförlag, Stockholm
www.raben.se
Translation copyright © 1995 by Rabén & Sjögren
All rights reserved
First published in 1992 by Rabén & Sjögren Bokförlag, Sweden
as *Nisse på stranden* © 1992 by Olof and Lena Landström
Library of Congress catalog card number: 95-067923
Printed in Italy
First American edition, 1995
First paperback edition, 2001

ISBN 91-29-65305-3

Will and Mama are going to the beach.

It's great to get going at last.

"I hope we didn't forget anything," says Mama.

I remembered my swim ring at any rate, thinks Will.

"I can smell the sea!" Mama calls out.

Will and Mama have arrived.

"Just the right-size waves," says Will.

"Let's practice swimming today," says Mama.

Will thinks the beach is crowded.

Suddenly big raindrops start to fall.

Will is cold but he still wants to test the water.

It's warm!

"Just think," says Mama. "You really swam!"
It's funny I didn't just sink, thinks Will.